Brian Wilds

My Dream

Oxford University Press
Oxford   Toronto   Melbourne

Oxford University Press, Great Clarendon Street, Oxford OX2 6DP

Oxford New York
Athens Auckland Bangkok Bogotá Buenos Aires
Calcutta Cape Town Chennai Dar es Salaam Delhi
Florence Hong Kong Istanbul Karachi Kuala Lumpur
Madrid Melbourne Mexico City Mumbai Nairobi Paris
São Paulo Singapore Taipei Tokyo Toronto Warsaw

and associated companies in
Berlin Ibadan

Oxford is a trade mark of Oxford University Press

© Brian Wildsmith 1986
First published 1986
Reprinted 1987, 1989, 1990, 1992, 1994, 1995, 1997, 1998, 1999

This edition is also available in
Oxford Reading Tree Branch Library Stage 2 Pack **A**
ISBN 0 19 272144 5

All rights reserved

British Library Cataloguing in Publication Data
Wildsmith, Brian
My dream.—(Cat on the mat series)
I. Title   II. Series
823'.914[J]   PZ7
ISBN 0-19-272161-5
USA ISBN 0-19-849008-9

Printed in Hong Kong

I go to sleep.

I ride a tiger.

I sit on a whale.

I lift an elephant.

I climb a giraffe's neck.

They all fly away.

But so can I.

Then I wake up.